FIELD GUIDE TO THE
GRUMPASAURUS

FROM THE NOTES OF

EDWARD HEMINGWAY

The observations that follow in this field guide tell you everything you need to know about the formidable *Badmoodicus grumpasauricus*, more commonly known as the North American Grumpasaurus.

CLARION BOOKS
Houghton Mifflin Harcourt
Boston   New York

Clarion Books
215 Park Avenue South
New York, New York 10003

Clarion Books is an imprint of Houghton Mifflin Harcourt Publishing Company.

www.hmhco.com

The illustrations in this book were done in oils on panel.
The text was set in American Typewriter Regular.

Library of Congress Cataloging-in-Publication Data
Names: Hemingway, Edward.
Title: Field guide to the Grumpasaurus / by Edward Hemingway.
Description: Boston ; New York : Clarion Books, Houghton Mifflin Harcourt, [2016] |
Summary: A field guide to the fierce but adorable grumpasaurus, found in every home
where there are small children.
Identifiers: LCCN 2015020006 | ISBN 9780544546653 (hardback)
Subjects: | CYAC: Temper tantrums—Fiction. | Behavior—Fiction. | Humorous stories. | BISAC:
JUVENILE FICTION / Social Issues / Emotions & Feelings. | JUVENILE FICTION / Humorous
Stories. | JUVENILE FICTION / Imagination & Play. | JUVENILE FICTION /
Animals / Dinosaurs & Prehistoric Creatures. | JUVENILE FICTION / Family / General
(see also headings under Social Issues).
Classification: LCC PZ7.H377436 Fi 2016 | DDC [E]—dc23
LC record available at http://lccn.loc.gov/2015020006

Manufactured in Malaysia
TWP 10 9 8 7 6 5 4 3 2 1
4500579090

For Mums

Special thanks to Ada Charlotte Case and
Nick Woods (a.k.a. Uncle Grumpy)

Curious about the world's most fearsome creature?

It's the GRUMPASAURUS!

Sometimes called Grumpelstiltskin or the Great Grumpsby, the Grumpasaurus can live anywhere, and is most often seen sulking around the room after a great tragedy or mishap. Such as . . .

a broken toy.

When the Grumpasaurus gets REALLY UPSET . . .

lightning will strike.

And thunder will roll.

Its nostrils will flare.

And the scales on its back will rise.

(They sure don’t make quality toys like they used to.)

Approach with caution.

Then fear its mighty ROAR!

And head for the hills.
Best to be curious about the Grumpasaurus
from a safe distance.

Much better.

When it's done sulking, the Grumpasaurus will always seek out the nearest adult, demand some attention, and get ready to speak its mind.

You may want to plug your ears . . .

. . . Grumpasauruses can be very loud.

What, exactly, is it trying to say?

No one knows for sure . . .

but everyone can hear it.

Yeesh! The Grumpasaurus sure can make a lot of noise.

GRUMP!
Its tears sound like pouring rain.
Its scales rattle up a storm.
Its VERY LARGE mouth hollers like there's no tomorrow.
Looks like it didn't brush today.
THUMP!
THUMP!
(So *that's* what its tail is for!)

If the Grumpasaurus won't settle down, even after an adult asks it to, drastic measures must be taken. Like . . .

. . . BATH TIME.

WARNING

The Grumpasaurus is at its most fearsome when being forced to do something it doesn't want to do. KEEP YOUR DISTANCE . . .

. . . or it will strike.

Splash!

You can't say you weren't warned.

It’s simply never a good idea to approach the Grumpasaurus, unless . . .

. . . bearing gifts.

HMMM?

Then it will say "Thank you" with a hug.

Awww.

Wait a minute.
The most FEARSOME creature
IN THE WHOLE WORLD gives HUGS?
It's true.
And there's one more very important thing you should know:

The moment it smiles . . .

. . . the Grumpasaurus disappears without a trace.

And you can approach at will.